This Book Belongs To:

Destini & Deirée Metcalf
1987

THE RAND McNALLY
BOOK OF Favorite
Bedtime Stories

RAND McNALLY & COMPANY ⊕ Chicago
Established 1856

This book contains the stories THE THREE BEARS VISIT
GOLDILOCKS, NUMBER 9: THE LITTLE FIRE ENGINE,
NOAH'S ARK, and TWILIGHT TALES, copyright © by
Rand McNally & Company in MCML, MCML, MCMLII and
MCMXLVII, respectively. 1978 Edition. Printed in U.S.A.

Library of Congress Catalog Card Number: 64—17442

CONTENTS

The THREE BEARS
Visit Goldilocks

ONE FINE DAY Mother Bear said to Father Bear, "Let's take Baby Bear to visit Goldilocks this afternoon."

So, after a quick lunch of honey cakes and porridge, the three bears set out for the little white cottage at the foot of the hill.

When they reached the cottage, no one was there because Goldilocks and her Mother and Father had gone for a walk.

Father Bear knocked at the door KNOCK! KNOCK! KNOCK! in a big loud knock. No one came.

Mother Bear knocked at the door KNOCK!
KNOCK! KNOCK! in a middle-sized knock.
No one came.

Baby Bear knocked at the door *knock!*
knock! knock! in a wee little knock. And lo
and behold! the door swung gently open. It
was not locked!

The three bears stared in surprise. Then Baby Bear poked his head in the door, just to take a peek.

"Oh, look, Mother! Goldilocks has three chairs, too! A big red leather chair. A mid-

dle-sized chair. And a wee red chair for Goldilocks."

The three bears tiptoed about the living room feeling the soft red chairs. But they did not sit in them.

Baby Bear poked his head into a big bedroom — just to take a peek. Then he poked
his head into a middle-sized bedroom. Then
he poked his head into a little bedroom.

"Oh, Mother! Goldilocks has three beds,
too! A big bed with a high pillow. A middle-

sized bed with a middle-sized pillow. And a wee little bed with a soft little pillow!"

At these words Baby Bear yawned and crept into the wee little bed with the soft pillow and was soon fast asleep.

When Baby Bear woke up a short time later and peeked into the big bedroom, he was surprised to find Father Bear sound asleep in the big bed.

Mother Bear was fast asleep in the middle-sized bed.

Baby Bear slipped quietly away and went exploring.

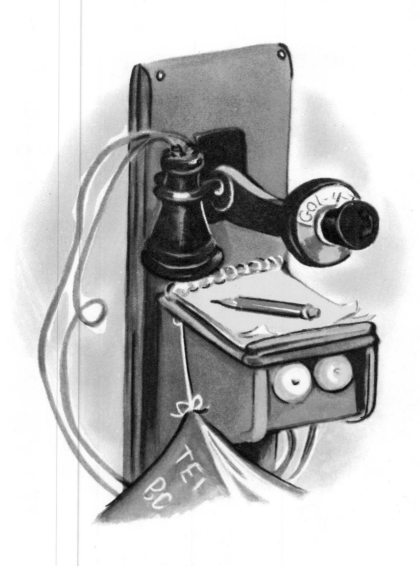

On the wall Baby Bear saw something. He did not know that it was a telephone. He reached up and took the receiver off the hook.

"Number, please," came a pleasant voice. "Number, please."

Baby Bear did not know what else to say, so he said "Three" because there were three in his family.

He heard a buzzing sound.

"HELLO!" came a deep voice. "Locker plant! Frozen fish, frozen fruits, frozen vegetables! What can I do for you?"

Baby Bear shivered. "*Brr-r*, it must be

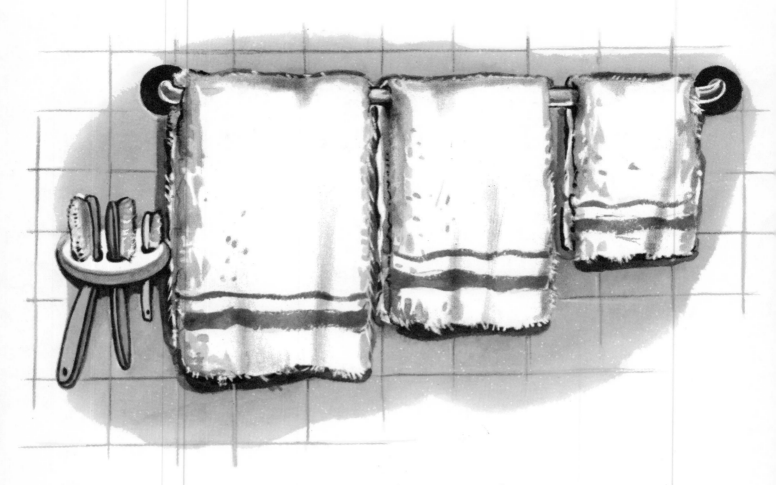

the North Pole. Everything's frozen up!" He put the talking thing back on the hook and crossed to a door which opened on a small room. Baby Bear did not know it was a bathroom.

Baby Bear saw a big white tub. He climbed in and sat there, looking around. As he started to climb out, he accidentally caught hold of the faucet and cold water splashed out all over him.

Baby Bear did *not* like that! He scrambled to get out of the tub and, as he did so, he twisted the faucet again and the water stopped.

Baby Bear rolled himself up in the rug to get dry.

After a while Baby Bear crept out and went to investigate a round blue thing on the wash basin. Baby Bear did not know it was a tube of tooth paste and that someone had left the cap off.

As he turned it around in his paw, he squeezed it too hard, and all at once

Splat! a gob of tooth paste hit him right in the left eye.

Baby Bear looked into the mirror at his one-eyed self. Oh, my! What a funny sight! He wiped away the tooth paste as best he could on a pretty towel hanging near by.

Just then his eye caught sight of something in a glass jar on the shelf. It was a beautiful golden color — just the color of honey! Baby Bear took it down and took a big taste. Oh, my! He did not know that it was shampoo for washing hair.

"Oh, oh, oh," he cried. And each time he opened his mouth to say, "Oh," a beautiful soap bubble floated out. It was wonderful.

Baby Bear stood before the mirror entranced and watched the little round bubbles drift forth as he made soft little "oh's." He watched until the beautiful bubbles stopped coming.

Just then a voice said, "*Coo-coo, coo-coo, coo-coo.*"

Baby Bear felt someone was laughing at him and he went to see who it was. He looked and looked, but he found no one calling, "*Coo-coo.*"

He did not know that it was the cuckoo clock over his head in the hall.

In the living room Baby Bear saw a large piece of furniture. He did not know that it was a radio set. He began to play with the buttons on the side. All at once a voice called out at him — "Strike one!"

"Oh, my! Strike me?" cried Baby Bear.

He turned the buttons every which way, trying to stop the voice. But, all at once, there appeared on a white screen above his head a man with a baseball bat. Baby Bear did not know that he had turned on the television.

He took one look at the man with the bat as the voice called, "Strike two" and raced for help.

Baby Bear pulled and tugged at Father Bear and woke him up. Then he pulled and tugged at Mother Bear and woke her up.

All three bears tiptoed to the living-room door and peeked at the screen.

The man with the bat swung furiously, and the loud voice boomed, "Strike three!"

The three bears rushed out into the kitchen and hid under the table, the white cloth almost covering them.

At this very moment Goldilocks returned with her father and mother.

As they came in the front door, Goldilocks said, "Someone has been looking at our television set!"

Then she went to the bathroom and looked at the tooth paste and shampoo and towel. "Someone has been in our bathroom!"

Then she looked into the bedrooms. "Someone has been sleeping in our beds."

As she turned around, she heard a noise in the kitchen and saw the table cover moving. Goldilocks' father said, "Someone is hiding under our table, and I know who it is. It is Father Bear and Mother Bear and wee Baby Bear."

At the sound of his voice the three bears scrambled out from under the table and lunged through the open door. They lumbered away up the hill toward home and never stopped till they reached their own little house in the woods. And Father Bear and Mother Bear never took Baby Bear to visit Goldilocks again!

NUMBER 9

The Little Fire Engine

NUMBER 9 was a Fire Engine in a big city. But he was a little fire engine and not new any more. And so the larger, newer engines had crowded him out of one big engine house after another. At last he came to stay in a little engine house way out on the edge of the city.

Old Jeff, Number 9's driver, went there with him. Old Jeff was one of the best firemen in all the city. He even had medals pinned on his coat because of his brave deeds. But now the Fire Chief thought that he and Number 9 were too old to be of much use at a big fire.

Number 9 did not like to sit in the engine house day after day without any work. Old Jeff did not like it, either. He used to talk to Number 9 when he was polishing his bright red paint and brass work.

"They think we're too old to be of any use," he would grumble.

"Don't fret," Number 9 would say to Old Jeff. "Our chance will come. Some day these new firemen and engines will have a fire too big for them. Then they'll have to call on us to help them out."

Months went by, and not once did the signal ring for them.

Then, early in the morning of the very coldest day of the year, a big fire broke out downtown.

Old Jeff and Number 9 listened to the signals that called for one fire engine after another.

"Will they call us this time, Number 9?" Old Jeff said. "They think we're too old to be of any use at a big fire. Perhaps they'll forget all about us again."

But this time Number 9 felt sure, clear down to the middle of his motor, that he and Old Jeff would be called.

"No, Old Jeff," he said. "They won't forget us this time. This fire is too big for those young firemen and new engines to handle by themselves. They'll have to call out us old-timers."

Just then the signal rang again. It was for them. Number 9 was right! He and Old Jeff were going to the big fire.

Whee-e-e-e! Old Jeff sprang into his seat. The broad doors of the little engine house swung open and Number 9 dashed out. He went so fast that the other firemen who rode on him hardly had time to put on their helmets and rubber coats and swing aboard.

Along the snowy streets roared Number 9.
"Oo-wee-oo-oo-oo!" squealed his siren. "Get out of
the way! Out of the way! We're going to the big
fire! Oo-WEE-oo-o-o!"

When they got downtown, Old Jeff could
see the clouds of smoke rolling up from the burning buildings. "It's a good thing we're coming,"

Old Jeff said to Number 9. "Do your best now,
Number 9!"

Soon they passed the fire lines, where police-
men were holding the people back so that the
firemen would have plenty of room to work.
Number 9 rolled up close to the burning buildings.

"The worst fire is in the Smith Building,"

Old Jeff said. "These new firemen don't know how to fight a big fire. They've forgotten all about the hydrant in the alley behind the Smith Building."

Just then the Fire Chief ran up. "You here, Old Jeff?" he cried.

"All here, both Old Jeff and Number 9," Old Jeff called back.

"You can help Number 40 with its pumping," said the Chief. "We need all the water we can throw, and more, too."

"The place for Number 9 is at the alley hydrant, behind the Smith Building," said Old Jeff.

"Too dangerous," said the Chief. "The walls may fall any minute. We need the water back there badly, but I won't order any man to go there."

"Ho-ho!" laughed Old Jeff. "Number 9 and I will give you all the water you want from the alley. Come along, Number 9."

When they came to the hydrant behind the Smith Building, Old Jeff spoke. "Here is where we stop," he told Number 9.

Old Jeff fastened his pumping hose to the hydrant. Number 9 pumped water as fast as he could pump. *Whee-e-e!* It was hard work, but Number 9 thought it was the most exciting thing he had ever done.

Old Jeff heard some bricks crash down near
by. He saw that the wall was ready to fall. He
filled another oil cup for Number 9 and then, just
in time, crawled under the little Fire Engine.

With a mighty crash the wall fell. Part of it fell on Number 9.

"Are you hurt, Number 9?" called Old Jeff from underneath.

"Not badly, Old Jeff," Number 9 called back. "I'm bent up a bit, and I'm afraid I shall burst my tires, the wall is so heavy. But my pump and my motor are not hurt. I can run for a long time yet. Are *you* hurt, Old Jeff?"

"Just my ankle, where a brick hit me," said Old Jeff. "But I think I still can crawl around and give you a little oil when you need it. We'll show them yet! Won't we, Number 9!"

After the wall fell, the water from the hose lines came over Number 9 more than ever. By and by, so much water had fallen on him, and on the heavy wall on top of him, that nothing at all could be seen of the little Fire Engine. Only a great lump of glittering ice stood in the alley where Number 9 had been.

After a long while the firemen had poured so much water on the flames that the fire was not a big one any more—only a middle-sized one. Soon it was not a middle-sized fire—only a small one. And then, at last, the Fire Chief had time to think about Old Jeff and Number 9. He ran down the alley to the back of the Smith Building. There he saw the great lump of glittering ice.

"Come quick!" he called to some firemen. "The wall fell on Old Jeff and Number 9. We must dig them out. Poor Old Jeff, he would risk it here!"

The firemen got tools and began to dig. In a little while one of them said to the Chief, "Do you hear that sound coming from under the ice and bricks?"

The Chief listened. "Why, it's old Number 9,

still pumping away!" he cried. "Hurry, boys! Perhaps Old Jeff is all right, too."

The firemen dug harder than ever. At last they came upon Old Jeff. He was crawling under the ice and broken wall, giving Number 9 another drink of oil.

The Chief was proud of Old Jeff and Number 9.

The people of the city, too, were proud of Old Jeff and Number 9. They pinned another medal on Old Jeff and they gave Number 9 a

new coat of bright red paint. They shined his brass work until it looked like gold and paraded him through the city to the biggest engine house.

And there he stands today, with a little brass plate on his side to tell visitors about his brave work.

Old Jeff stays at the big engine house, too.

He takes care of Number 9 and keeps him shining. But they are willing now to stand aside and give younger firemen and fire engines a chance. After all, they went to the worst fire the city ever had. And, as everyone knows, not a fireman or a fire engine there did more than brave Old Jeff and faithful Number 9.

NOAH'S ARK

Once upon a time, they say,
The rain came down, day after day.

So Noah built a boat so wide
That all the Animals
could stay inside.

Listen to their noisy din!
Look! Each one of them has a twin.

Up the gangplank . . . onto the Ark,
The bossy Cows moo
    and the little Dogs bark.

The Pigs were hungry
    and got there first,
Their manners always
    are the worst.

Flipping and flopping,
  the clumsy Seals
Came aboard with noisy squeals.

The Camels looked
  very wise and proud;
"Hump-h," said one,
  "it's quite a crowd!"

The Lions arrived with kingly air,
Bag and baggage . . .
    going somewhere!

The Giraffes, of course,
 had the best view,
But then Giraffes
 most generally do.

Two prancing Ponies,
   with shiny coats,
Wondered where Noah
   had put the oats.

Two little gray Squirrels
scampered away
Hiding nuts for a rainy day.

The little brown Bears
    watched with glee
A spouting Whale out in the sea.

And it's lucky that
    a Duck can swim,
For with a splash—one tumbled in!

Two naughty Foxes
        were hiding about
Busily thinking up trouble, no doubt!

The Tigers looked like
great big kittens,
But can you imagine them
losing their mittens?

"So many strange faces,"
    sighed the Peacock in blue;
"Do you know them, Sir Owl?"
He blinked and said, "Who-o?"

A pair of Doves as white as snow
Circled above the crowd below.

Soft and woolly,
     two little white Sheep
Huddled together . . .
     oh, where is Bo-Peep?

Two little Rabbits
    hopped down the lane,
Bringing umbrellas
    to keep off the rain.

Leaping high,
    having heard the news,
Over the hill came the Kangaroos.

The Hippos had to squee-e-e-ze
through the gate,

Huffing and puffing . . .
and terribly late!

All aboard! 'Twas just about dark,
When the Animals sailed away
safe on the Ark!

Twilight Tales

MRS. HEN'S RED HAT

MRS. HEN had three butter-yellow chickens. They lived in a cozy little coop behind the plum tree.

One day Mrs. Hen said to her children, "I wish I had a nice, gay, red hat!"

"Well, Mother, if you want a red hat, you should *have* one," said Cheery Chick, who was a pleasant little fellow with snapping black eyes.

"You get food for us when we are hungry and you cuddle us under your warm wings when we are cold," said Chatty Chick, who could talk the best.

"And when we go outdoors, you walk slow so that I can keep up," said Chubby Chick, who was the smallest.

"Well, then, let's go shopping for a hat," said Mrs. Hen, looking pleased.

She took some pieces of golden corn money out of the pink sugar bowl, and they started out.

They went first to the Fieldmice's Underground Department Store which was a hole in the ground. It had a flat door over the top of it, and on that was written:

"PLEASE KNOCK, SCRATCH, PECK,
OR THUMP."

Mrs. Hen pecked.

The door flew open so quickly that it whacked her on the end of her bill, and the three little chickens tumbled over backward. But no one minded. They even laughed a little, especially Cheery Chick.

Mr. and Mrs. Fieldmouse looked out of the hole.

"Do you happen to have a nice, pretty, red hat?" Mrs. Hen asked them.

"Oh, we are so sorry," said Mr. Fieldmouse. "We have only gray raincoats and mud-rubbers and little bright firefly lanterns for dark cellars."

"That's too bad," said Chatty Chick. "Mother does *so* want a red hat."

"Well, where shall we go now?" sighed Chubby Chick. He was getting a wee bit tired.

"To Mrs. Owl's Shop in the hollow tree," his mother said. "She is so wise that I feel sure she will keep red hats."

Mrs. Owl looked very gray-and-white and sleepy. She had an apron on.

"Do you happen to have any red hats?" Mrs. Hen asked her.

"I'm very sorry, but I just keep night reading glasses, black bandages to wind around your eyes so you can go to sleep in the daytime, and loud hoot whistles."

"This is very disappointing," said Mrs. Hen. "I did so want a red hat, and we have looked just everywhere. We are very tired from shopping."

"Or trying to shop," said Chatty Chick.

Mrs. Owl looked very wise. Her eyes grew big as butter plates. Then she said, "Why don't you all go home, have a nice cup of tea and maybe some cookies, and think it all over?"

"That is just what we will do," decided Mrs. Hen. "It is a very good suggestion, Mrs. Owl."

So they all trooped home to the cozy little coop
behind the plum tree.

"Too bad," said the chickens as they had their
tea.

But all of a sudden Cheery Chick brightened
up. "Why, Mother," he said, "you do have a
red hat, all the time!"

"What do you mean?" asked Mrs. Hen.

"The red comb—the one you have on the top
of your head—"

"Oh, but that grew on me," said Mrs. Hen.

"But it makes a lovely hat," said Cheery Chick.

"If you just think of it that way," added Chubby.

Mrs. Hen looked at herself in the mirror. "And you don't think I need another hat?" she asked. "One I could put on—and take off—whenever I wished?"

"Oh, Mother, we like you just the way you are!" the chickens said. "You have red hat enough for us! And you look so beautiful in it!"

Then Mrs. Hen put the pieces of golden corn money back into the pink sugar bowl. She said to her three little butter-yellow chickens, "Well, then, everything is all right! I have you and you have me, and we have saved our money. So let's be happy just as we are, a fine feather family in our cozy little coop home behind the plum tree."

THE BIG NOISE AT HALF-PAST THREE

MRS. SQUIRREL lived up high in a treehouse.

One day she looked at her little clock and thought, "It is nearly half-past three. My little boy Timmy will soon be coming home from school."

She hummed a little leafy tune.

But suddenly there was a big, big NOISE. It

shook the treehouse and clinked the dishes and tipped a flowerpot over.

"Oh, mercy me, what was that?" wondered Mrs. Squirrel. Then she heard footsteps down below.

"Who's that stepping on my stair?" she called out.

"It's the grocer-boy squirrel with the nuts. Did you hear that big noise? The tall dead tree in the forest fell over!"

"So *that* was it," said Mrs. Squirrel.

The grocer-boy squirrel put the bag of nuts on the table. "I dropped the groceries when the big noise happened," he said. "They spilled all over the grass. I thought a bad animal was after me."

"But you're all right now," said Mrs. Squirrel. "Here, have a piece of caraway cake."

After the grocer boy had gone, there were more footsteps down below.

"Who's that stepping on my stair?" called Mrs. Squirrel. "Timmy—it must be you! I was so excited over the big noise that I forgot to look at the clock. It is nearly four!"

"No, it's not Timmy," quacked a voice. "It's me—Mrs. Duck from the Cat-Tail Swamp. I was putting on my little orange hat when there came a big noise. I jumped so that I pulled my hat 'way down over my eyes, and it is stuck tight. I can't get it off. All I can see is my feet!"

"Come up and I will help you," invited Mrs. Squirrel. She gave the little orange hat a pull, and off it came.

"The big noise was the tall dead tree in the forest," Mrs. Squirrel told her. "It fell over. Here, have a piece of caraway cake."

Mrs. Duck ate her cake. Then she went home. Soon the clock struck four. Then Mrs. Squirrel was worried!

"Why," she thought, "school lets out at half-past three—and Timmy is not here yet. I must go and look for him."

She skittered to the forest thinking Timmy had gone to look at the fallen tree. But Timmy was not there.

"Oh, where is he?" sighed Mrs. Squirrel.

She ran to Grandmother Grump's house. Grandmother Grump was a ground hog. She was old and wise and kind.

"Oh, Grandmother Grump, I am having such a time," Mrs. Squirrel told her. "First, there was that big, frightening noise at half-past three. And, now, Timmy isn't home from school yet!"

"What time does he usually get home?" asked Grandmother.

"At quarter of four."

"Well, it is half-past four now. Why don't you go home and see if he is there? He may have come while you've been away."

Mrs. Squirrel ran home.

"Who's that stepping on my stair?" called a voice, and little Timmy came running down! Mrs. Squirrel hugged him, and they went upstairs.

"Did you hear that big noise at half-past three?" each one asked. Then they both laughed.

"But why didn't you come right home from school the way I have always told you to?" Mrs. Squirrel asked Timmy.

"I *did* come right home from school."

Just then there were footsteps down below. "Who's that stepping—" began Mrs. Squirrel, but a voice said, "It is Miss Meadow Rabbit, Timmy's teacher. I wanted to see if Timmy got

home all right. Just at half-past three there was a big noise—"

"The tall dead tree in the forest fell over," said Mrs. Squirrel.

"And when the noise was finished, I looked at the clock, and it was not half-past three any more—it was only three."

"The noise must have shaken the hands of the schoolroom clock," said Mrs. Squirrel. "Was that it?"

"Yes, that was what happened. So I kept the children till the hands got around to half-past three again, for that is the time school lets out. But, of course, that made them late—"

"Then Timmy did come right home from school after all!" said Mrs. Squirrel. "I am so glad!"

"I came right home," smiled Timmy. "I told the truth."

"Yes, you did," said his mother. "But what an afternoon we have had! The big noise made all kinds of queer happenings for us little animal people.

"It tipped my flowerpot over. It spilled the

groceries. It pushed Mrs. Duck's hat 'way down over her eyes. It sent the hands of the clock back half an hour. And it made the children late home from school!"

"But all that is over now," said Timmy.

"Indeed it is," laughed his mother. "Miss Meadow Rabbit, will you stay and have some caraway cake with us? It's only a quarter of five—"